ISBN: 979-8-9851897-3-5 Hardcover

ISBN: 979-8-9851897-4-2 Paperback

Library of Congress Control Number: 2024900448

THE ONE AND ONLY ME!
AN AFFIRMING BOOK FOR CHILDREN

STORY BY:
PETIKA TAVE

ART BY:
VIKAS U.
K. VIGN

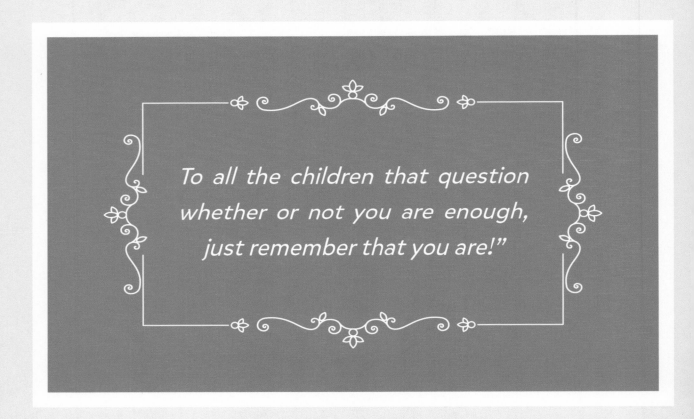

To all the children that question whether or not you are enough, just remember that you are!"

_____

is the proud owner of this book!

When I wake and look in the mirror each morning

there is nothing better to see

than the amazing, **brilliant,** totally cool—

One and Only Me!

When I think of how **wonderful** I am,
from my head down to my feet,
I am **proud** of who I see staring back—
it's the **One and Only Me!**

I love that I'm **healthy** and **strong**,
such important things.
I also have a **brilliant** smile,
I love the **joy** that it brings.

Thinking of what I love about myself,
the list is far from small.

I love that I help those in need,
that I'm **friendly** and **kind** to all.

I have many **gifts** and special **talents**
like drawing, dancing, and more.
I love thinking about what lies ahead
and what for me is in store.

There are days when I don't feel so great,
but I **try not to be down for long.**

When I'm ready, I **hold my head up high,**
I love how it helps me feel **strong.**

Sometimes at school kids say mean things and ignoring them just won't do,

so I walk away, then tell an adult—
I know that's the right thing to do.

Occasionally I might feel afraid
or scared to say how I feel,
that's when I go to someone I trust,
so they can help me to **heal.**

It's OK not to have all the answers.
I'm still a kid, I know.
But what's important is that I see

my experiences will help me grow.

All the traits that make me special and all the things I go through,

have created the unique person I am.
There's no limit to what I can do!

Regardless of what I see around or what's popular on TV,
I still love how I'm made because
I'm the **One and Only Me!**

I love my eyes, my hair, my nose, my smile, my laugh, and my walk. My hobbies, my goals, my strengths, and my struggles— I'm **thankful** for them all.

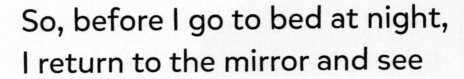

So, before I go to bed at night,
I return to the mirror and see

no matter what the day has brought...
I'm still the **One and Only Me!**

Discussion Questions

1. What do you love **most** about yourself? Why?

2. What special **talents** do you have? (Note: Everyone has something, even if you don't know what it is yet.)

3. What **skill** would you like to develop?

4. Explain what the phrase "The One and Only Me" means to **you.**

5. Choose someone close to you. What would they say are **qualities** you possess?

Discussion Questions

(6) **Who inspires** you? Why?

(7) **What inspires** you? Why?

(8) If someone tries to make you feel bad or "less than," what are ways you can handle that?

(9) Is there anything you would like to share about yourself that people may not know?

(10) Who can you talk to if you are not feeling your best? (We're talking about emotions, not illness.)

Affirming Activities

① Affirming words: Write 5 words that **best** describe who you are.

② List three things you are **proud** of.

③ List two things you are **good** at.

④ Write one sentence that **best** describes what you love most about yourself.

Create a Collage!

Write it down!

Directions:

Think of all the things that make you unique. Write a paragraph or two that describes those qualities and what you love about yourself the most. Share and discuss with your parents/guardians and let them tell you what they love about you too!

_____

_____

_____

_____

_____

_____

_____

About the Author

PeTika Tave is part of the mom and daughter team that makes up BayaBooks and More, which stands for "Beautiful and Brilliant As You Are" Books and More. She, along with her daughter Zandria, is dedicated to making sure all children love themselves, inside and out, just the way they are. Through her struggles with self-esteem as a youth, her passion is to affirm children and strengthen families by creating resources and literature that help equip parents and adults with what they need to address the social-emotional needs of children. Couple that with her over 19 years of experience in the classroom, her passion for literacy and children can be seen through her work in the community and the products she creates. To learn more about the work of PeTika and her daughter, visit their website at www.BayaBooks.com. You can also follow them on social media to gain valuable knowledge and resources, in addition to reaching out for school visits and community events. Never forget, "you are beautiful and brilliant, inside and out, just the way you are!"

@authorpetika   @bayabooks

Made in the USA
Columbia, SC
13 October 2024

43518850R00022